THE NEWS ABOUT
DINOSAURS

THE NEWS ABOUT

DINOSAURS

BY PATRICIA LAUBER

BRADBURY PRESS

NEW YORK

The author would like to thank Dr. Donald Baird, Director
Emeritus of the Museum of Natural History at Princeton University,
for his thoughtful comments and generous help.

Page 1: *Yangchuanosaurus* attacks *Mamenchisaurus*, a long-necked sauropod. Illustration by Gregory
S. Paul © Gregory S. Paul 1988. Page 2: *Hypacrosaurus*, a duck-billed dinosaur, has brought food to her
young in their nest. Illustration by John Gurche © John Gurche 1987. Page 4: Young *Brachiosaurus*
traveled with the herd. Illustration by Gregory S. Paul © Gregory S. Paul 1988.

First American Edition   10 9 8 7 6 5 4 3 2 1

LIBRARY OF CONGRESS CATALOGING-IN-PUBLICATION DATA
Lauber, Patricia.   The news about dinosaurs.
Summary: Discusses all of the latest scientific thinking about dinosaurs, with illustrations keyed to
major topics.   Includes index.
1. Dinosaurs—Juvenile literature.   I. Title.
QE862.D5L46   1989   567.9′1   88-24140
ISBN 0-02-754520-2

HOW TO SAY IT

Albertosaurus—al-BER-tuh-sawr-us

Allosaurus—AL-uh-sawr-us

Apatosaurus—ah-PAT-uh-sawr-us

Archaeopteryx—ar-kee-OP-ter-ix

Barosaurus—BAR-uh-sawr-us

Baryonyx—BAR-ee-ON-is

Brachiosaurus—BRAK-ee-uh-sawr-us

Brontosaurus—BRON-tuh-sawr-us

camarasaur—KAM-uh-ruh-sawr

Camarasaurus—KAM-uh-ruh-sawr-us

camptosaur—KAMP-tuh-sawr

Ceratosaurus—sair-AT-o-sawr-us

Chasmosaurus—KAZ-muh-sawr-us

Coelophysis—see-lo-FISE-iss

coelurosaur—see-LURE-uh-sawr

Deinonychus—dyne-ON-ik-us

Diplodocus—dih-PLOD-uh-kus

gorgosaur—GOR-guh-sawr

Hypacrosaurus—hi-PAK-ruh-sawr-us

hypsilophodont—hip-sih-LO-fuh-dont

Iguanodon—ig-WAN-oh-don

Lagosuchus—lah-go-SOOK-us

Lewisuchus—lew-ee-SOOK-us

Maiasaura—mah-ee-ah-SAWR-uh

Mamenchisaurus—mah-MEN-chee-sawr-us

Nanotyrannus—NAN-o-tie-ran-us

pterodactyl—tair-uh-DAK-til

sauropod—SAWR-o-pod

Triceratops—try-SAIR-uh-tops

tyrannosaur—tye-RAN-uh-sawr

Tyrannosaurus—tye-RAN-uh-sawr-us

Yangchuanosaurus—yang-CHEW-anno-sawr-us

By courtesy of the British Museum (Natural History)

Baryonyx Walkeri

J.W.Holmes - 1986 -

▶ *Baryonyx* was 30 feet long, with 15-inch claws and a snout like a crocodile's. It probably lived along rivers and used its claws and snout to catch fish. It was discovered near London, England, by a plumber whose hobby was searching for fossils, traces of ancient life preserved in rock. *Baryonyx* means "heavy claw."

Dinosaurs were discovered in the early 1800s. Until then, no one had even guessed that once there were dinosaurs.

Scientists studied the big teeth and bones they had found. They wondered what kind of animals these belonged to. Finally they decided the animals were reptiles—relatives of today's crocodiles, turtles, snakes, and lizards. In 1841 the animals were named *dinosaurs,* meaning "terrible lizards."

Dinosaur hunters dug for bones. They found giant dinosaurs, dinosaurs the size of chickens, and many in-between sizes. They gave each kind a name. They fitted bones together and made skeletons. After a hundred or more years, this work seemed to be ending. Scientists began to think they had discovered nearly every kind of dinosaur that ever walked the earth.

THE NEWS IS:

The work was far from finished. Today new kinds of dinosaurs are found all the time. And scientists think there must be hundreds more that they haven't discovered yet. Four of the new kinds they have found are *Baryonyx, Mamenchisaurus, Deinonychus,* and *Nanotyrannus.*

8

▶ *Mamenchisaurus* was a giant plant-eating dinosaur, 72 feet long. Its 33-foot neck is the longest of any known animal. The dinosaur is named for the place in China where it was found.

▶ *Deinonychus* was found in Montana. It was fairly small, about 9 feet long, and walked on its hind legs. Each hind foot had a big claw, shaped like a curved sword. The dinosaur's name means "terrible claw." Like other meat-eaters, *Deinonychus* spent much of its time resting or sleeping and digesting its last meal. This pair has just awakened, hungry and ready to hunt.

▶ *Nanotyrannus* was a pygmy tyrannosaur, a small relative of *Tyrannosaurus rex*. Its name means "pygmy tyrant." This small meat-eating dinosaur looked like its big relative but was only one-tenth as heavy and one-third as long—it weighed about 1,000 pounds and was 17 feet long. *Nanotyrannus* was discovered in a museum, where it had earlier been mistaken for another meat-eater, a gorgosaur, also known as *Albertosaurus*. Here its jaws are about to close on a smaller dinosaur.

By Robert T. Bakker

Most reptiles walk with their knees bent and their feet wide apart. Scientists used to think dinosaurs must have walked the same way. They pictured dinosaurs as slow and clumsy, waddling along with their tails dragging on the ground. So that was how dinosaurs were made to look in books and museums.

▶ For many years, people thought of dinosaurs as slow-moving and slow-witted. That is how they appear in this 1870s painting by Benjamin Waterhouse Hawkins. He was the first artist to work closely with scientists who were studying dinosaurs.

THE NEWS IS:

Dinosaurs didn't look like that at all. They were good walkers. They held their tails up. And many kinds were quick and nimble. Today's scientists have learned this by studying dinosaur footprints.

When dinosaurs walked in mud or wet sand, they left footprints. Most of these tracks washed or oozed away. But in some places the tracks hardened. Later they were buried under mud or sand that turned to rock. The tracks were preserved in the rock—they became fossils.

▶ Today dinosaurs are shown as lively and active. These huge, horned plant-eaters are driving off *Albertosaurus*, a fierce meat-eater.

Tracks show that dinosaurs walked in long, easy strides. Their legs and feet were under their bodies, not out to the side. Their bodies were high off the ground. Big plant-eaters walked at 3 or 4 miles an hour. Some small meat-eaters could run as fast as 35 or 40 miles an hour.

By Douglas Henderson © (in cooperation with Martin Lockely)

▶ Camarasaurs (foreground) and camptosaurs are crossing a recently flooded area and leaving footprints. Preserved in rock, such tracks have revealed much about dinosaurs.

▸ At least some dinosaurs could swim. *Apatosaurus* has tried to escape a pack of *Allosaurus* by taking to the water—but the meat-eaters can swim, too.

In the 1870s a famous dinosaur hunter discovered a huge skeleton. The bones had belonged to a plant-eating dinosaur that was 65 feet long and weighed 35 tons. The scientist named it *Brontosaurus*.

There was just one problem. The skeleton had no head. The scientist had to guess what the head had looked like. His guess was a big head with square jaws and a blunt nose. Later a skull like this was mounted with the body. *Brontosaurus* became one of everybody's favorite dinosaurs.

THE NEWS IS:

The head and body did not belong together. The skull belonged to *Camarasaurus*. The body belonged to *Apatosaurus*, a kind of dinosaur that had been found and named before the dinosaur hunter discovered the big skeleton.

Most museums have now put an *Apatosaurus* head on their skeletons. They have also changed their signs. They use *Apatosaurus* because it is an older name for the dinosaur than *Brontosaurus*. But many people still use the name *Brontosaurus* to mean a giant, plant-eating dinosaur.

By Joyce Powzyk

▶ *Camarasaurus* had a big head, with square jaws and a blunt nose. Dozens of peg-shaped teeth edged its jaws. *Apatosaurus* had a much smaller head, which was long and slender. Its small spoon-shaped teeth were at the front of its jaws.

The biggest dinosaurs belonged to the group of plant–eaters named sauropods. Among them were *Mamenchisaurus, Diplodocus, Brachiosaurus, Apatosaurus,* and *Camarasaurus.* They were the longest, tallest, heaviest land animals that ever lived. They had legs like tree trunks, long tails, and long necks that ended in small heads.

Earlier scientists thought these giants spent their lives in shallow lakes or swamps, where water helped support their heavy bodies. Some scientists wondered if sauropods were able to walk on land at all.

THE NEWS IS:

Sauropods were very much at home on dry land. They may have spent some of their time in water, but they didn't live there. Their bones and footprints have been found in places that were dry part of the year and rainy part of the year. They have been found in places where forests of evergreens grew in the days of dinosaurs.

Footprints show that sauropods walked in long strides on all four feet. They may have reared up on their hind legs, using their tails for balance, to feed from the tops of trees.

Giant animals need giant amounts of food. A large sauropod must have eaten several hundred pounds of plant food a day. Perhaps sauropods traveled about, following the greening of forests as rainy seasons came and went.

▶ Sauropods were at home on dry land, where they used their long necks to reach into treetops for food. Shown here are *Camarasaurus* (left), *Barosaurus* (center), and *Apatosaurus* (right).

▶ Like all sauropods, *Brachiosaurus* (left) and *Barosaurus* (right), moved easily on land, which was helpful when they met meat-eaters such as *Ceratosaurus* (center).

▶ Sauropods probably traveled long distances to new sources of food.

Today's reptiles do not live in groups. They do not hunt together. They do not feed together. Males and females come together to mate, but the rest of the time they live alone. And so, for many years, scientists thought that was how dinosaurs had lived.

THE NEWS IS:

Many dinosaurs banded together in herds and in packs or pairs.

Footprints show that small meat-eaters hunted in pairs or packs. So did medium-sized meat-eaters. Big meat-eaters hunted in pairs or alone.

Tracks also show that many plant-eaters lived in small herds. They fed together and gathered around water holes.

Some of these footprints are like snapshots. They catch dinosaurs in action, millions of years ago. Tracks in Australia, for example, tell of a stampede. A herd of plant-eaters had been milling around together. Suddenly they all turned in one direction and ran. Another set of footprints tells why. They are the tracks of a meat-eating dinosaur, and they appear on top of the tracks made by the fleeing herd.

The bones of adults and young are sometimes found jumbled together in one place. These remains are another sign that plant-eaters lived in small herds. One day the dinosaurs were feeding or moving about. Something happened, and the whole herd died. Perhaps it was caught in a flash flood and drowned. Perhaps it was killed by a mudflow from an erupting volcano.

▶ A pack of *Allosaurus* attacks *Diplodocus,* which probably depended on its great size and whiplike tail to protect itself.

▶ Two *Tyrannosaurus* hunt for prey, while pterodactyls circle overhead, waiting for a chance to feed on remains of the kill.

In the same way, large numbers of bones show that small herds sometimes joined together, forming one huge herd. One day a herd of 10,000 duck-billed dinosaurs was thundering along in what is now Montana, perhaps on their way to new feeding grounds. Something happened, and they were all killed. Today their bones are scattered over an area two and one half miles long and a quarter of a mile wide.

By Douglas Henderson ©

▸ Flash floods, caused by great storms, may have wiped out herds of dinosaurs.

Most of today's reptiles do not take care of their young. The young find their own food. No adult protects them from animals that want to eat them. Scientists used to think dinosaurs did not take care of their young, either.

THE NEWS IS:

At least some dinosaurs do seem to have cared for their young. They seem to have tended the young and guarded them.

When dinosaurs were on the move, the young traveled in the middle of the herd. There, they were surrounded by adults and protected from meat-eaters. Footprints tell this story.

▶ Footprints preserved in rock show that when sauropods moved around, their young were kept at the center of the herd.

▶ Horned dinosaurs may also have lived in herds and protected their young. Here *Triceratops* defends its young against *Tyrannosaurus*.

Other signs show that some kinds of dinosaurs guarded their eggs and young. Duckbills seem to have brought food to their young.

Eighty million years ago, a shallow sea ran north-south through North America. Bones show that herds of *Maiasaura,* a duck-billed dinosaur, lived on low-lying plains near the sea. When they were first discovered, the bones were puzzling. They were all the bones of adults. Why, scientists wondered, were there no baby duckbills or eggs?

After a while, they found the answer. Duckbills did not lay their eggs on the low-lying plains. Instead, they used nesting grounds that were miles away, on higher, drier land. The same grounds were used year after year by colonies of duckbills.

At the nesting grounds, females spaced themselves out. Each dug a bowl-shaped nest and laid her eggs in it. The spaces between nests are exactly the length of one duck-billed dinosaur.

The nesting grounds hold the remains of nests, eggs, young duckbills, and adults. The adult bones show that duckbills did not simply lay their eggs and go away. They stayed with their eggs and young and probably guarded them.

▶ *Maiasaura* females banded together in colonies at their nesting ground.

28

▶ *Maiasaura* parents guarded their eggs and their young.

Scientists think that baby duckbills could not feed themselves. Eggshells in the nests are crushed. This is a sign that the young stayed in their nests. As they moved around, they broke and crushed the shells, as baby birds do. Also, scientists have been taking X rays of unhatched dinosaur eggs. Some of the eggs have tiny dinosaur skeletons inside. Duckbill skeletons show that these dinosaurs developed slowly in their eggs. They do not look as if newly hatched young could scramble out of the nest and feed themselves.

Yet the teeth of very young duckbills are worn from chewing. The wear marks tell scientists that the young ate berries, grasses, and seeds. If the young stayed in their nests, then adults must have brought them food. Adults must have fed their young, just as many kinds of birds do today.

Not far from these nesting grounds are ones used by other dinosaurs. Among them were the speedy, nimble hypsilophodonts. In their nests only the top half of the eggshells is broken. These young seem to have left their nests after hatching. X rays of one kind of hypsilophodont egg show a well-developed tiny dinosaur. Like today's reptiles, these young may have hatched out ready to find their own food.

Bones show that young hypsilophodonts stayed in the nesting ground until they were half-grown. Adult bones are a sign that parents may have guarded their young until they could run fast enough to escape enemies.

▸ Hypsilophodont young were apparently ready to leave
the nest soon after hatching.

All of today's reptiles are cold-blooded. Their bodies do not make much heat. To be active, reptiles need an outside source of heat—sunlight, warm air, sun-warmed water. When reptiles are cool, they are sluggish and slow-moving.

Mammals and birds are warm-blooded. They make their own heat, and they can be active by day or by night, in warm weather or in cool. They have much more energy than reptiles do and can stay active for hours at a time.

Scientists long thought that dinosaurs, like today's reptiles, were cold-blooded animals.

THE NEWS IS:

Some dinosaurs may have been warm-blooded. *Deinonychus*—"terrible claw"—is one of those dinosaurs.

Deinonychus was fairly small. It had the sharp teeth of a meat-eater, hands shaped for grasping prey, and powerful hind legs. It also had a huge, curved claw on one toe of each hind foot. This was a claw shaped for ripping and slashing.

To attack, *Deinonychus* must have stood on one hind foot and slashed with the other. Or it must have leaped and attacked with both hind feet. Today's reptiles are not nimble enough to do anything like that. And as cold-blooded animals, they do not have the energy to attack that way. Warm-blooded animals do. That is why some scientists think *Deinonychus* must have been a warm-blooded dinosaur. They also think that many of the small, meat-eating dinosaurs were warm-blooded.

▸ Three *Deinonychus* work together to bring down *Iguanodon,* which was too old or too sick to defend itself with its thumb spike or tail.

Perhaps other dinosaurs were, too. One clue may be the rate at which they grew.

Warm-blooded animals grow much faster than cold-blooded ones. A young ostrich, for example, shoots up 5 feet in a year. A young crocodile grows only about 1 foot.

Bones in the nesting grounds of Montana show that duckbills were 13 inches long when they hatched. Scientists think young duck-bills were 10 feet long at the end of their first year. If that is right, it is a sign of an animal that grew fast—perhaps of a warm-blooded one.

▸ Young duckbills seem to have grown fast.

By Douglas Henderson ©

▸ Large dinosaurs must have kept moving in search of food. Some scientists say this is a sign they were warm-blooded—otherwise they would have lacked the energy for long marches. Other scientists say that big dinosaurs didn't need to be warm-blooded. They lived in a warm climate. They made heat by using their muscles. And their huge bodies were able to store large amounts of heat.

By Douglas Henderson © (collection of Museum of the Rockies)

rchaeopteryx is the oldest known bird. It lived about 150 million years ago, during the age of dinosaurs. About the size of a crow, *Archaeopteryx* had wings and feathers. It had a wishbone, a kind of bone that is found only in birds. But in every other way, *Archaeopteryx* looked like one of the small meat-eating dinosaurs that ran on two legs. It had the bones, claws, teeth, and long tail of a dinosaur.

How could this strange creature be explained? Some of the first scientists to study it thought they knew the answer: Birds had developed from dinosaurs. Today's birds must be descended from dinosaurs.

Later scientists decided this idea was wrong. They could not find any dinosaurs that looked like close relatives of *Archaeopteryx*.

▶ *Archaeopteryx* chases down a lacewing insect. Notice the legs of sauropods behind the tree trunks.

THE NEWS IS:

Many scientists now feel sure that birds did develop from dinosaurs. They say that dinosaurs did not entirely die out. Instead, some of their descendants became the robins, crows, eagles, and other birds we see today.

The close relatives of *Archaeopteryx* seem to be the coelurosaurs, small meat-eating dinosaurs. Their skeletons are a good match for *Archaeopteryx*.

At some time, scientists say, small changes began taking place in a group of coelurosaurs. Over millions of years, the small changes added up to big ones. Reptile scales, which are like feathers in certain ways, became feathers. Arms, hands, and fingers grew into wings. Collarbones joined to form wishbones. A group of dinosaurs had become birds.

By Douglas Henderson © (collection of Ruth Hall Museum of Paleontology)

▶ *Coelophysis* is one of the small meat-eating dinosaurs that may be close relatives of *Archaeopteryx*. So is *Deinonychus*.

Some scientists think there may also have been dinosaurs with feathers. Suppose, they say, small meat-eating dinosaurs were indeed warm-blooded. Body heat escapes quickly from small animals. Feathers would help the body keep its heat. They would serve as insulation. So perhaps the scales of these dinosaurs developed into feathers.

Perhaps they did, no matter how strange it is to think of dinosaurs with feathers.

▶ *Deinonychus* and other small meat-eaters may have had feathers.

D inosaurs ruled the earth for 140 million years. During that long time, many kinds of dinosaurs died out. New kinds took their place. Then, around 65 million years ago, all the dinosaurs died out. So did many other kinds of life.

No one knows for sure what happened. But in the last days of dinosaurs, great changes were taking place on earth. Shallow seas dried up. Ocean levels dropped. Volcanoes erupted. Mountains rose from plains, and swamps became high, dry land. With these changes came another. The climate cooled, all over the world.

Perhaps the earth changed so much that dinosaurs could no longer live on it. For many years, that was what most scientists thought.

▶ Over 140 million years many kinds of dinosaurs developed. One of the earliest kinds was *Lewisuchus,* which is shown here eating *Lagosuchus,* another early dinosaur, which was about 1 foot long.

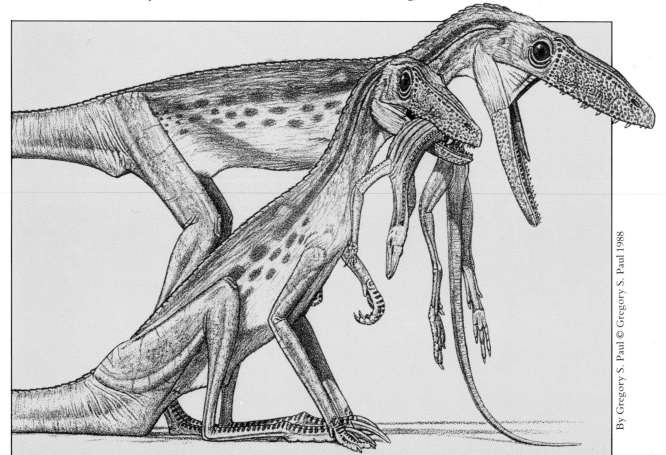

▸ One of the last kinds to develop was *Chasmosaurus,* a horned dinosaur with an enormous neck frill.

THE NEWS IS:

A cooling, changing earth may not be the whole answer. Scientists have found a clue that something else may have played a part in the great dying-out.

The clue is an odd layer of clay. It has been discovered in a hundred places, all over the earth. It is always found sandwiched between rocks that are 65 million years old. The clay is rich in a material called iridium. The earth has iridium, but most of it is buried deep inside our planet. Iridium found near the surface has usually come from space. It comes to earth in meteorites.

Most meteorites are chunks of comets or asteroids. They plunge into the earth's atmosphere and light up the sky before they strike the ground. Really big meteorites blast craters in the earth's surface.

Many scientists think the iridium-rich layer of clay formed after the earth collided with a giant meteorite or a swarm of smaller meteorites. The collision hurled huge amounts of dust and iridium into the air. Winds carried dust and iridium around the world. The dust was so thick that it shut off the sun's light for weeks. In this time of ever-night, green plants died. Plant-eating animals starved to death. So did animals that hunted and ate other animals.

In time the dust settled out of the air, becoming a layer of iridium-rich clay. The sun shone on a much-changed earth, an earth without dinosaurs.

▶ Iridium can also come from deep inside the earth. It reaches the surface when volcanoes erupt. Some scientists think that huge eruptions were taking place 65 million years ago. Clouds of ash choked plant and animal life. Dust and iridium rose into the atmosphere, shutting off the sun's light, and later formed the iridium-rich layer of clay. Volcanic eruptions, these scientists say, were what wiped out the dinosaurs.

By Douglas Henderson © (collection of Museum of the Rockies)

Early dinosaur hunters discovered that many kinds and sizes of dinosaurs once roamed the earth.

Today's dinosaur hunters are discovering how dinosaurs lived—how they moved and traveled and fed and defended themselves. They are learning what dinosaurs were like before they hatched. They are even learning about dinosaur senses and voices.

The part of a skull that holds the brain is called a braincase. It shows the size and shape of the brain. It shows which parts of the brain were highly developed. In dinosaurs these parts were ones that receive information from the senses. Dinosaurs had good eyesight and a keen sense of smell. They also had a keen sense of hearing.

By Douglas Henderson © (collection of Phil Tippett)

▶ Dinosaurs were alert. Their keen senses helped meat-eaters to find prey and plant-eaters to learn of danger.

By Eleanor M. Kish. Courtesy of the National Museum of Natural Sciences, National Museums of Canada

▸ Most dinosaur skin rotted away after the animals died. So we may never know what colors dinosaurs really were. But scientists feel sure that dinosaurs did have markings of various colors, just as today's animals do. Stripes, for example, would have helped a duckbill to blend into the broad-leaved forest, making it hard for a meat-eater to see. Meat-eaters may have had markings that helped to conceal them when they stalked their prey.

By Douglas Henderson © (collection of Phil Tippett)

▸ A splash of color would call attention to the spiny neck frill of this horned dinosaur, which may have frightened meat-eaters.

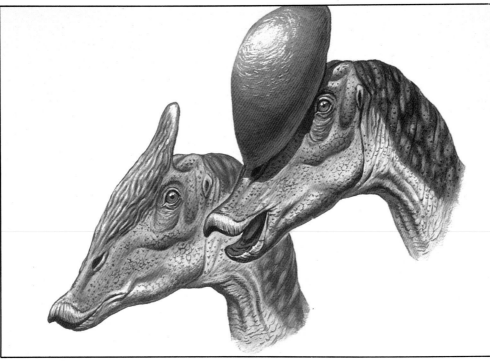

▸ Some dinosaurs may have had hollow pouches on their heads, which could be blown up and used to scare off enemies or to attract mates.

Still other bones show that dinosaurs had voices. Young dinosaurs may have squeaked and squealed. Bigger dinosaurs may have croaked, tootled, barked, bellowed, bayed, or made sounds like a tuba.

With all the new discoveries, perhaps it seems there's not much left to learn about dinosaurs.

THE NEWS IS:

Scientists will be finding new dinosaurs and learning about dinosaur lives for years to come. And when they do, their discoveries will be reported in the news.

INDEX

Illustration references are in **boldface type**.